LOVE LETTERS

A nine week Study Guide based on Psalm 119

By Joe Castillo

ARTSTONE
PUBLISHERS

130 4th Street
Fayetteville, GA 30214
ArtStone@me.com
LoveLetters@JoeCastillo.com

LOVE LETTERS - THE STUDY GUIDE
Published by ArtStone Publishers, LLC

© 2022 by Joe S. Castillo.
International Standard Book Numbers
Hard Back: 978-0-9840459-4-5
Soft Back: 978-0-9840459-5-2
eBook: 978-0-9840459-6-9
Study Guide Soft Back: 979-8-223-73197-9
Study Guide eBook: 979-8-223731-9-79

Library of Congress Number: 2022905104

Cover Design and all artwork: Joe Castillo

For information on special discounts, bulk purchases and live programs contact:
ArtStone Publishers
LoveLetters@joecastillo.com

10

Unidades.

LOVE LETTERS

A nine week Study Guide
based on Psalm 119

By Joe Castillo

ARTSTONE
PUBLISHERS

130 4th Street
Fayetteville, GA 30214
ArtStone@me.com
LoveLetters@JoeCastillo.com

Contents

◊ ◊ ◊

Hello.

(Uhm, hi)

I wrote a book for you.

(Thanks, what is it about?)

It is about a young woman who goes looking for real love and finds her true mission in life.

(I wish I could figure out how to do that)

That is why I wrote it. This story can help you. Will you read it?

(I don't read much, but OK.)

Good, I am excited for you.

◊ ◊ ◊

(Hey, that was a pretty cool story. I read it all in a week. I cried at some parts.

Did you really write it for me?)

Yes I did. Thank you. Would you like to know my secret reason for writing it?

(You had a secret reason?)

Yes, my secret reason was to get you to read Psalm 119, the longest chapter in the Scriptures. You did that.

(What? When?)

The words that Beth wrote is the entire 22 chapters of Psalm 119.

(How cool. I am going to have to go back and read it again.)

Reading and following the words of Scripture will change your life.

(I need that. My life is so screwed up.)

Mine was too. I know the Words of God changed me. That is why I wrote this study guide. To help you understand how it works.

(I already read the book, why do I have to do a study guide?)

Just like Beth in the story, you have a journey to go on.

(Well... I guess. I don't have anything else to do but text someone. So boring.)

Great. You start by reading this introduction.

It is the shoes you will walk in for this journey.

(I don't want to read the introduction, introductions are boring.)

Read the introduction. It will not be boring. It is like being barefoot and being given the best pair of sneakers you ever had. Give it a try.

(Fine, just this once I'll try it.)

INTRODUCTION

Read this before the first meeting

The best way to really get something valuable and lasting out of the book 'Love Letters' and Psalm 119 is to follow this study guide.

    1. Read the book 'Love Letters.'

    2. Follow the study guide for Psalm 119.

    3. Meet weekly with friends to discuss it and encourage each other.   4. Discuss the questions at your own level.

    5. Share your needs so others can pray for you and pray for others.

    6. Write thoughts to God in your Journal as you study on your own.

The Scriptures:

    Studying the Scriptures can be like a continual feast.

    We have to eat every day to grow and be healthy.

    We need daily spiritual food too.

    What God promises in His Words is spiritual nourishment. A steady diet of study and application helps us grow, overcoming discouragement, depression and help smooth out the damaging highs and lows of life. Young women have been reading, studying, meditating and living-out these God-Words for thousands of years.

It really is a packet of 'Love Letters' God has given to his people. They are 'Love Letters.' Some written to you but all written for you.

◊ ◊ ◊

(You really mean, like Love Letters God wrote specifically for me?)

Yes. That is exactly what I am saying. Just like the Prince wrote Love Letters to Beth, God wrote His Love Letters for you. I promise, if you look in God's Word for spiritual food included just for you, you will find it. You can even learn to share spiritual meals with others. Maybe your boyfriend or "Mr. Right", when he comes along.

(I haven't ever fixed a real meal for myself, don't have a boyfriend much less a "Mr. Right", although I like the idea.)

Reading and learning the Scriptures can even help with finding 'Mr. Right.'

(You are kidding right!?).

Nope. I have seen it happen.

THE STUDY GUIDE:

This study guide can be worked through on four levels.

1. What it says. You can read the Scriptures and discover the basic meaning and have a discussion about a love story like 'Love Letters' that follows a young woman's growth in her faith and develops confidence to discover how deeply she is truly loved. You... yes **You, can discover that God really loves you!**

2. Why He wrote it. If you want to learn more, ask the questions that reveal why God wrote a passage and understand the life-changing power of God's eternal words. **You will understand why God loves you and why He wants to change you from the inside.**

◊ ◊ ◊

(Can God really do that? My step-dad always said, 'you're worthless, you ain't never gonna change.')

He is wrong. God can change anyone. Even your step-dad. *(I would have to see that to believe it!)*

Believe it.

3. How it applies to you. Then you might go a bit deeper and find the underlying meaning that makes it all work. That is getting in to the 'how' of it. How did God use writers, poets and prophets to say and write what they did. Find out how God made you. **Find out how you are supposed to live? You can find out what important mission God wants you to fulfill.**

(Now that would be a good thing to know. I don't have a clue.)

I have seen it work in hundreds of lives. Mine included. And last of all:

4. What you can learn about Him. For those with a sincere love, there is a peek into a deeper friendship with God. When you really know Him through the deliberate study of His words and obedience to them, you begin to understand some of the underlying meanings of this ancient and foundational book that God used to root the faith of His chosen people. You can even memorize some of those verses. Spending time in His Words, is spending time with Him. In this sweet study of His precious Words you will discover that a friendship with God is enough. **You will know that walking with Him is more fulfilling, satisfying and wonderful than any relationship on earth.**

◊ ◊ ◊

See, you made it all the way through the introduction. Congratulations!

(So like, I read about what can happen. Now do I get see if it really works?)

You bet. What was your favorite part of the 'Love Letters' book?

(It was all cool. The part I liked best was when she whips that Belial dude's butt.)

Me too. So, do you think The Scriptures are really that important?

(Like really, are they more important than what I wear to school tomorrow?)

Yes. If you know the Scriptures and apply them honestly to your life, the benefits are huge. It will determine how much you want to learn and how deep your friendship with God will be.

(Now do I get a new pair of shoes?)

Absolutely, let's try them on.

WEEK ONE - God wants you on a firm Foundation

Psalm 119:1
Words, Symbols, Provision, Heart

Read this aloud:

PRAYER: *"Lord, I pray that I can find happiness by learning to follow what you say."* **Vs. 1**

1   THE WORDS

In Psalm 119 the first letter of each line in that eight verse section uses the next letter of the Hebrew alphabet. It is called an acrostic. Any verse or song where each line starts with the same letter is an acrostic. You cannot see it in your english Bible but if you could read ancient Hebrew you would see it. Our word 'Alphabet' came from the first two letters in the Hebrew, Aleph-Bet. Not only that, the poet/scribe mentions 'The Words of God' in <u>every single one</u> of all 176 verses.

◊ ◊ ◊

I call her my 'Glad Girl.' Some would say she had a difficult childhood. Her parents divorced shortly after she was born. Her father never had any interest in her and she was raised by a single mom. But my wife, Cindy was given her own printed copy of God's Words when she was fifteen.

At first Cindy was overwhelmed by the Scriptures with its strange stories, people from ancient history and confusing messages from God.

What Cindy discovered is that no other book in the history of the world is like it. It is amazing. It is supernatural. It is miraculous. What these words did for Cindy was help her get to know God, gave her confidence and became life long guidance and support. One day she heard about something called the 'Glad Game' where you look for something to be 'Glad' about. When she would go through really hard times she would write lists of things to be glad about. Today, fifty years later, her first copy of the Scriptures is tattered, underlined, ink stained, taped together and full of notes. Knowing it and living it filled her with peace and a joy that has lasted her entire life. She still plays the 'Glad Game' almost everyday.

◊ ◊ ◊

(Oh, is that why you call her your 'Glad Girl')

Yup. And she is.

Do you have a have a printed copy of this amazing book? If you don't, email me and I will send you one at no charge. LoveLetters@joecastillo.com

(For free!? You would really do that?)

Yes, that is a promise.

The Scriptures are able to transform you. They can give you the tools to know how to live a life filled with 'Love, Joy, Peace, Patience, Kindness, Meekness, Gentleness and Self Control.

(Is that really true?)

Guaranteed!

Ideas to talk about:

1. What do you think convinced Beth to trust the words of the Prince?
2. Have you ever been encouraged by a passage from the Words of God?
3. What would convince you that you are loved by God?

2   THE SYMBOLS

Other than a history of God and His people, and direct communications from Him, the Bible could be seen as an instruction manual for planet earth. It helps when we learn what symbols or word pictures the Bible uses to describe itself. Here are at least twelve different items the Scripture points to.

Take turns reading each of these symbols aloud to your group.

1. Milk - is nourishment for new believers.

"you need someone to teach you… the basic principles of God's words. You need milk, … because everyone needs to start out on milk which is the good news about righteousness." (Hebrews 5: 12-13)

2. Solid Food - a hearty meal for healthy growth.

"The Solid food of the word is for the mature, who by regular study and training have learned to distinguish good from evil." (Hebrews 5:14)

3. A Sword - a weapon for defense from attack and spiritual surgery.

"Therefore put on the full armor of God,... and take up the sword of the spirit which is The Words of God..." (Ephesians 6:11, 17)

The sword is also described as being 'living' and able to slice open the thoughts and motivations of our hearts. *"The word of God is alive and powerful, sharper than any sword, ..., to discover the thoughts and intentions of the heart. (Heb. 4:12)*

4. A Shield and Hiding Place - For protection and safety.

"You are my hiding place and my shield. I hope in your Word." (Psalm 119:114)

5. Fire - Intended for purification.

The prophet Jeremiah describes the Words of God as a fire. *"But if I told myself, 'I am not going to mention his word or even talk about God, his word is blazing in my heart like a fire, a fire shut up in my bones."* (Jeremiah 20:9)

6. A Hammer - a tool to demolish and destroy.

Jeremiah also speaks of God's word as a hammer.

"My words are... like a hammer that breaks the rock in pieces?" (Jer. 23:29)

7. A Mirror - an honest evaluation

James uses a mirror to illustrate the revealing nature of the Words of God.

"The person who studies their reflection in the perfect law of God, that gives freedom, and lives their life accordingly, will not forget what he has seen and heard, but does it." (James 1:23-25)

8. A Seed - that gives new birth and the source of growth.

The Word of God is compared to seeds that won't die when they are planted.

"You have been born all over again, not like a seed that will die, but eternal. Born through the living and lasting word of God." (1 Peter 1:23)

9. A Lamp - light for direction and understanding.

The Word of God is compared to a lamp.

"Your words are a lamp that shows me where to walk, and a light that shines on my path." (Psalm 119:105)

10. Water - for refreshment

The Word of God is described as water, an essential source of life.

"Just like rain and snow fall from above… and waters the earth, producing seed giving plants and bread to eat." (Isaiah 55:10-11)

10. Honey - sweetness and strength.

According to the writer of the psalms, the Scriptures are sweeter than honey.

"The judgments of the LORD are true and righteous altogether. More to be desired are they than gold, sweeter also than honey and the honeycomb." (Psalm 19:9,10)

11. Gold - provides wealth and status.

"Because I love your commands more than gold, more than pure gold, and because I consider all your precepts right, I hate every wrong path."
(Psalms 119:127-128)

12. An Anchor - gives stability and security in a storm.

We are told that God's words are like an anchor for our soul.

"We have a great hope, a secure and steadfast anchor for our soul," (Heb.6:18,19)

These word pictures, or symbols, that the Bible gives to describe itself are very helpful in our understanding of the importance of the Word of God.

Ideas to talk about:

1. Which of the symbols listed above did Beth use on her journey?

2. What symbol would be most helpful to you right now?

(I sure could use some of that gold, but the sword would be helpful in defending myself against my brother.)

I don't think God would want you chopping up your brother with his Words.

Read this section aloud:

3 THE PROVISION

Psalm 119 is one of the most fascinating, intriguing and inspirational chapters in the entire Bible. The main theme is 'The Words of God.'

Within its 176 verses God says His Words can restore you in times of failure; purify when caught in sin; correct when you are wrong; show the truth when you are lied to; given victory when you have been defeated; songs during times of failure; hope in times of doubt; relief during pain; direction home when you are lost; make you thankful; give you a helping hand when you are weak; set you free when you are judged; honey to appease your hunger; light for the darkness; a safe place when you are afraid; encouragement from the one you serve; wonder in a drab world; holiness when you have been polluted; an advocate when you are condemned; peace in the midst of turmoil; and most of all a shepherd to lead you into an eternal home. Psalm 119 tells us that to know the Creator God you must know His word, it is the transformational power for life.

Ideas to talk about:

1.   **When did Beth begin to find hope in the Love Letters?**

2.   **Have you ever read a part of God's Words that encouraged you?**

Read this aloud:

 **THE HEART**

The greatest benefit of reading and knowing God's Words is listed in the first two verses of Psalm 119. The writer tells you that you can be happy. (In the Scriptures, 'blessed' or in the original language 'Shalom,' means to be happy, peaceful or content.) *"Happy are those who do what is right, who follow what the Lord says, who follow him with all their heart." Ps. 119:1*

This is an amazing promise. If you remember, Beth kept coming back to the Letters again and again. As we grow in our love for God we will learn to follow Him. This is always a heart issue. The first eight verses of Psalm 119 really deal with the issue of the heart. Who or what do you love? If we love someone, we will follow them. There are four kinds of hearts listed in these passages:

1. An Undivided Heart: Vs. 2 "Those who "joyfully obey His laws and search for it with their whole (undivided) heart." This means obeying completely. Not holding anything back. It is putting all our choices before Him for His approval.

2. A Faithful Heart: Vs. 4 *"You have charged us to keep your commandments carefully."* To be careful, implies choosing wisely and being faithful with how we keep His commands daily.

3. An Attentive Heart: Vs. 7 *"As I learn your righteous regulations I will thank you by living as I should."* Learning comes from paying careful attention, listening and applying what we have heard.

4. An Obedient Heart: Vs. 8 *"I will obey your decrees. Please don't give up on me."* Responding to every desire and whim of our God, will give us an obedient heart. Will you pray that God will change your heart?

Ideas to talk about:

1. **How did Beth's heart change as the story progressed?**

2. **What finally brought her to have the right kind of heart?**

3. **Can you ask God to give you a pure heart?**

◊ ◊ ◊

(I don't really don't think I can do that. My heart is so full of anger and hate.)

I really understand. I still struggle sometimes to let God change my heart. What I finally realized was that His grace was the only thing that could do it.

(Did he do it? Change your heart, I mean?)

Oh Yes, He has. When I come to the end of myself and trust Him to do it He does. Every time.

(I am right there. If he can't do it, I'm doomed.)

Ask Him. He will.

Preparations for next week:
- **Read & think about Psalm 119: 1- 8 (Chapter: Aleph)**
- **Can you pray that God will give you a pure heart?**

PRAYERS, DREAMS AND HOPES:

WEEK TWO - God knows your Name.

Psalm 119 verse 1- 8 (Letter: ALEPH)
Your Value, Your Name. A New Name, God's Name

PRAYER: *"LORD, help me obey your words. Please never give up on me." Vs. 5*

Read this aloud:

YOUR VALUE

Her name was Yu Cidu. In her country women were only valued for their beauty. It was of critical importance to be thin, have a smooth complexion, perfect make up and have tiny feet. They were starved, had their faces scrubbed with pumice stones, covered with makeup and then there was the problem of the feet. Big feet were considered ugly. Baby girls had their feet wrapped with canvas strips for years to keep them from growing too big. The pain was so excruciating, the baby girls would cry all the time. A select group of girls called geishas were trained to please men. They were really treated like honored slaves.

Yu was very young when she was sold by her parents into this service. As a young woman she was given a copy of God's Words. She read how Jesus treated women with respect, loved and lifted up the ones who had fallen. In Psalm 119 she read *"I will praise you sincerely as I learn from you the right way to live." Vs. 7.*

She also read about how God had made her just the way He wanted her to be. *"You Lord, created me and made me just the way I am." Vs. 73.*

Those Words changed her life. She believed God had made her a masterpiece and became A 'Woman of the Word'. After escaping from slavery she went on a journey to share the good news that took her all over the world. It was a journey of giving away copies of God's Words and telling thousands and thousands of women they were a special masterpiece. A unique work of God. They could believe that God had made them and loved them exactly the way they were. That truth would set them free.

Ideas to talk about:
1. **When did Beth begin to accept how God had made her?**
2. **Can you believe that God has made you a masterpiece?**
3.

(I don't feel like much of a masterpiece.)

Most young women do not believe it but it is true. Remember this also, God is not finished with you yet.

(That story about Yu Cidu was terrible. Or maybe a great one. Is it true? Was Yu real?)

(Yes she was. She was a hero to an entire generation of women in China.)

2 YOUR NAME

Is your name important? My best friend in elementary school hated her name. "Cigueña" in Spanish means "swan". It is a beautiful bird but my friend hated the name. So about every other week she would show up at school and announce to anyone who would listen that her name was Maria, or the next week it would be Sylvia or Victoria. If someone called her "Cigueña" she would ignore them. It also really hurt her mother who had chosen the name for her.

I read recently that when girls are kidnapped or trafficked, their abductor always changes their names and never uses their real name again. Not only does it separate them from their family but it also dehumanizes them. It makes them feel worthless.

I lost track of "Cigueña" but thought of her often. When one of my classmates was organizing a school reunion, I asked about her. The story I heard was that she had been married for thirty seven years. The young man that became her beloved husband, won her heart one day in the college library. He wrote; 'Will you marry me?' on a paper napkin and underneath drew two swans that formed a heart. She never complained about her name again.

As you have noticed, the text of Psalm 119 becomes part of the story of the 'Love Letters' which captivated the heart of a young girl looking for her identity, her purpose in life and true love. As

Beth pours out her soul in response to the 'Love Letters,' she carries with her, what she writes on the blank pages in her book is the text of Ps.119.

Her love for the Prince grows because of the Letters he wrote to her. She doesn't realize that the Prince is Aleph, walking beside her and caring for her every step of the way. Did you notice that her first attempts to write to the Prince are hesitant? She is a little nervous that it might not all be real.

Ideas to talk about:
1. **Beth in Hebrew means "house". Do you think she ever missed her home?**
2. **Do you know what your name means?**

(Wow, I love that story about swan girl. My step-dad still calls me 'hey stupid.')

That is very cruel of him to do that.

(Do you think that I could change my name?)

Yes you could, but I have some great news for you. There is something special about your name that you will learn about in the next segment.

3   YOUR NEW NAME

Many of the people in the Scriptures had their names changed and the meanings were also changed, which literally changed their lives. Here are just a few of those whose names God changed:

1. **Abram** - meaning "father" (although he had no children) had his name changed to **Abraham,** which means "father of many nations", (Gen. 17:5) and he was.

2. **Sarai** - meaning "princess", had her name changed to **Sarah,** "mother of nations" (Gen. 17:15) and that is exactly what she became.

3. **Jacob** - meaning "fake or substitute", was changed to **Israel,** "the winner". He even wrestled with God and won! (Gen. 32:22-28)

One of the beautiful messages in God's writings is that He has a secret name for you. He keeps it hidden, written on a white stone. He will reveal it to no one but you. Here is what He says: *"I will give you a white stone with a new name written on it, that only you will know." (Revelation 2:17)*

You already have a new name given to you by God!

Ideas to talk about:
1. Has anyone ever given you a pet name?
2. What special new name do you think God might give you?

(Wow! That is the coolest thing I have read yet. I know it won't be 'hey stupid.')

I can guarantee it won't be that. It will be something so special, it will change your life like it did all the others who were given a new name.

(I was a "premie", only 3 lbs 7 oz. when I was born. Mom called me "peanut".)

That is cute. I am sure that she loved you.

(Maybe. She gave me up for adoption when I was two years old.)

God said that earthly mothers may give up their babies but He never does. *"A mother may forget her baby but I will not forget you!" Isaiah 49:15)*

GOD'S NAME

God's name is important. 'Love Letters,' is also a story tied to an ancient and mystical alphabet called 'Hebrew' that was used to write most of the old section of the Scriptures. Back in the day they called it the 'Torah.'

God uses many different names for Himself in the Scriptures. In Psalm 119 we find only two names God decreed as His own. The first name of the Creator God: YAHWEH , (His personal name), often pronounced in English, JEHOVAH, means "the God who saves you, or God our rescuer". The second name is: ELOHIM. (His official title) like a CEO or King, or the President.

There are many other names used for God in His book. One of the most beautiful studies in the entire volume of God's Words is examining the Names of God and why they are used.

Here is a list of ten of them.

1. Jehovah Jireh: The LORD our provider (Genesis 22:14)

2. Jehovah Rapha: The LORD our Healer (Exodus 15:26)

3. Jehovah Nissi: The LORD our Banner (Exodus 17:15)

4. Jehovah Shalom: The LORD our Peace (Judges 6:24)

5. Jehovah Raah: The LORD our Shepherd (Psalms 23:1)

6. Jehovah Tsidkenu: The LORD our Righteousness (Jeremiah 23:6)

7. Jehovah Shammah: The LORD is Here (Ezekiel 48:35)

8. Abba Father (Daddy): Adopted, we cry out, "Abba! Father!" (Romans 8:15).

9. El Roi: "The God who sees me" (Genesis 16)

10. Elohim: "Supreme one" or "Mighty one". (Genesis 1:1)

Ideas to talk about:
1. **Did you pick up on the meanings of any other names in Love Letters?**
2. **Which of God's names would be most valuable to you right now?**

(I like Abba.' Is it OK to call God, Daddy?"

Yes, It pleases God when we are personal with him.

(Hey, thanks, I am really starting to get into this stuff.)

Great! I am excited for you. Remember the goal in learning about the Words of God is to get to know Him. He is the one who loves you with an everlasting love.

Preparation for next week:

- **Read and think about Psalm 119: 9 - 16 (Chapter: Beth)**

- **Pick out a verse that you can memorize for next week.**

- **Write the verse in your journal and some thoughts about God**

PRAYERS, DREAMS AND HOPES:

WEEK THREE - God wants you to know His Words.

Psalm 119: 9 - 16 (The Letter: Beth - בּ)
Study, Enjoy, Memorize, Share

PRAYER: *"LORD, help me remember your words so I won't sin against you." Vs. 11*

Read this aloud:

 **STUDY**

Fanny Crosby wrote more than 9,000 poems and songs. For most people, the most remarkable thing about it was that she was blind. An uninformed doctor accidentally prescribed a treatment shortly after birth that destroyed her vision. A few months later, Crosby's father died. Her mother was forced to find work as a maid to support the family, and Fanny was mostly raised by her grandmother.

In her very first poem written at age 8, made it clear that she refused to feel sorry for herself:

Oh, what a happy soul I am, although I cannot see!

I am resolved that in this world contented I will be.

How many blessings I enjoy that other people don't,

To weep and sigh because I'm blind I cannot, and I won't!

While still a young woman someone was expressing pity on her blindness and she answered by saying "If at my birth I had been able to make one petition, it would have been that I was born blind."

What transformed Fanny and kept her from feeling like a victim was her close walk with God and profound study and meditation on His Words. Shortly before her fifteenth birthday, Fanny was sent to the recently founded New York Institute for the Blind, which would be her home for 23 years: 12 as a student, 11 as a teacher. By age 23 Fanny Crosby was speaking at Congress and making friends with Presidents and royalty. A famous musician named Alexander van Alstine, married Crosby in 1858 and enjoyed writing the music to many of Crosby's hymns.

She continued to write and memorize Scripture up till the day she died at ninety five years old.

Ideas to talk about:
1. **How did Beth get to know the words of the Prince?**
2. **Do you know any verses of Scripture by heart?**
3. **What can you do to learn God's Word?**

◊◊◊

(Yikes, I have trouble remembering my own phone number.)
It would surprise you how much you could memorize with God's help.
(I love that story. I wish I could have met her)
Someday you will.

2   ENJOY

As we have discovered, Psalm 119 is a poem, an acrostic and was also written as a song. God specifically wants us to Love and enjoy His Words. Beth began to really appreciate the Love Letters and enjoy reading them both in the hard times and the good times. When we realize that Psalm 119 was actually a song, the lyrics can begin to change our entire outlook on life. We don't know what the song sounded like but we know that music can be a huge influence.

So much of what is recorded and played through our earbuds is negative and depressing. We often allow music to separate ourselves from our family, friends and most sadly from God. It can be a way of hiding. But there are thousands of songs hymns and spiritual songs that can bring us closer to God. He can speak to us through music, especially music that is taken directly from His Words. The Psalmist claimed that His Words: "had been music to my ears wherever I have lived." Vs. 54. And of course, Psalm 119 is a song that you can really love. We read that the writer: Enjoyed His Words more than money. Vs 14 and took pleasure in following His Words. Vs. 16

Ideas to talk about:

1. **Who sang songs that touched Beth's heart ?**

2. **Can you think of any songs or music that would draw you closer to God**

Have you ever gotten a song or piece of music stuck in your head? *(Oh yeah. some songs I really hate but I am finding all kinds of new songs that have God's Words in them. They touch my heart.)* So glad to hear that. Music is a wonderful way of drawing close to God.

3   MEMORIZE

One of the most amazing things about Fanny Crosby was her memorization of the Scriptures sometimes committing five chapters a week to memory. By age fourteen, **Fanny could recite the entire 176 verses of Psalm 119.**

There are many ways of learning the Words of God by heart. Songs using God's words is one way of doing it. In Psalm 119 verse 11 the writer says, "I keep what you say in my heart (memorize) so I won't sin against you. Thank you Lord! Teach me what to do! I repeat out loud your instructions."

His memorization plan is to:

- Study: "I will think deeply about your teachings." Vs. 15
- Reflect: I "reflect on your ways." Vs. 15
- Enjoy: "I will take pleasure in following your directions" Vs. 16
- Remember: Repeat often. "I won't forget what you say." Vs. 16

Here is a tip: Write out a verse on a card and put it somewhere you can see it often like your mirror. Reflect on what it means to you. Enjoy reading it aloud every day for a week. Each time say more of it from your memory.

Ideas to talk about:
1. **When was Beth really helped by having some of His Words memorized?**
2. **Can you think of any verses you might have memorized?**

4 **SHARE**

When we are close to God, he becomes a continual part of our lives. He gives us a desire to share His wonderful affirming, life changing and valuable truths with others. Unfortunately we get busy, distracted or fearful of sharing with others.

Four things that keep us from knowing and sharing God's Words.

1. **Criticism:** Even though some people make fun of us, it is not something we should ever do. "Even princes sit down together and make fun of me," Vs. 23

2. **Discouragement:** Depression and feelings of failure. " I'm weeping because I'm so sad; please encourage me," Vs. 28

3. **Lying:** We should not deceive ourselves about what is true. "Keep me from lying to myself; kindly teach me your law." Vs. 29

4. **Money and worthless things:** Material possessions like houses, cars and clothing, distract us. "Don't let me focus on things that are worthless." Vs. 37

Ideas to talk about:
1. **When did Beth start sharing The Words of the Prince with others?**
2. **Have you ever shared a verse or 'God moment' with someone?**

◊◊◊

Have you ever gotten a song or piece of music stuck in your head?

(Oh yeah. some songs I really hate but I am finding all kinds of new songs that have God's Words in them. They touch my heart.)

So glad to hear that. Music is a wonderful way of drawing close to God.

Did you try writing a verse on a card trick?

(Yes, Wow, that really worked for me!)

Way to go!

Preparation for next week:
- **Read & think about Psalm 119: 17 - 40 (Letters: Gimmel, Daleth, Hei)**
- **Find someone you can share good words with.**
- **Write some of your prayers and thoughts to God in your journal.**

PRAYERS, DREAMS AND HOPES:

WEEK FOUR - God wants you to follow Him.

**Psalm 119: 17 - 40 (Letters: Gimmel - ג, Daleth ד -, Hei - ה)
Discover, Understand, Trust and Follow**

PRAYER: *"LORD, please open my eyes so I many discover wonderful things in your Words."* Vs. 18

Read this aloud:

 **DISCOVER**

Her mind was made up. When she decided something, everyone knew it was a done deal. Escaping from a wretched, abusive family life became her first priority. She was going to commit suicide. A medical book from the school library had explained what pills and how many would kill her. She had taken them from her mothers bedside table. Tuesday night was the night.

Patty didn't know God. She had never been to church. No one had ever explained how much God loved her and the wonderful things He had for her. That very afternoon a classmate she did not know well, invited her to a gathering of God followers I was teaching. The invitation she had turned down many times before caused her to rethink her plan. 'I can always do it when I get home tonight' she thought.

That is how she discovered for the first time from God's amazing Words about His love for her and His willingness to lead her on the right path. The verse she heard was Psalm 119:18 "Open

my eyes so I may discover all the wonderful things in your words."
She desperately wanted to be happy. Her prayer was simply; 'God, please open my eyes.'

As soon as she got home she put the pills back into her mothers dresser, began reading God's Words. She not only discovered the truth, she understood the good news of His provision, trusted him and decided to follow. She never considered suicide again.

I know the story of Patty well. My best friend Danny shared it with me. after he Patty were married.

◊◊◊

(I have to admit, I have thought about that before.)
The rest of the story is the best part.
(I know. I pray it never enters my mind again.)
Patty and her husband have continued to discover more about God and his Words for more than forty years.

Ideas to talk about:
1. **What did Beth discover about Aleph?**
2. **Have you discovered something new about God?**

2 UNDERSTAND

Being willing to dig. *"Help me to understand what your laws mean, I will think about the wonderful things you do." Vs. 27* Dr. Sandra L. Richter is one of the smartest woman I know. She taught a Bible class that I sat in when I was in Seminary. The Book of Psalms was one of her favorite sections of God's Words and she really knew what she was talking about. What she said really helped understand.

"The Psalms have a unique place in the Bible because the Psalms speak for us. This is the ONLY book in the Bible that is written for instant application for you. No filter. This is the one book you can flip open and start praying whatever you see. This book was designed for that. No barrier between an ancient broken heart and a modern one; no barrier between us and God. Indeed, the Psalms <u>pray for us</u>. What a true and powerful word. Here the ancients remind us of who God is, who we are, and why we're going to make it through whatever it is we're dealing with this week. We hear the voices of the "great cloud of witnesses" who are pulling back the curtain on their own experiences to encourage us. Sometimes these voices are celebrating, sometimes angry, sometimes afraid, sometimes despairing. But the raw reality of their pain, their praise, and their faith makes us strong."

Ideas to talk about:
1. **When did Beth really begin to understand the Love Letters?**
2. **When you read difficult Scriptures do you skip over them?**
3. **What can you do to really understand the Words of God?**

3   TRUST

Everybody eventually has someone in their lives that fails them. Perhaps you have been disappointed, lied to or betrayed. We loose faith. Our ability to trust is damaged. Usually the damage is done by someone who has a piece of our heart. A lovely young woman I know well, named Christie told me the story about why she got a tattoo.

She began really liking a young man she was dating who had multiple tattoos. He told her he loved her and promised he would be faithful to her forever. To prove his love he was was going to get yet another tattoo with her name and suggested she get one too with his name. She trusted him.

It wasn't long before Christie's boyfriend was gone. Scorned and insulted he told lies about her and left. The tattoo was still there. It is much easier to get one than to have one removed. It is also much harder to trust after you have been betrayed.

With a broken heart Christie turned to God for healing and discovered that He was trustworthy. She could trust Him.

 FOLLOW

A rich art patron named John Ruskin after seeing her artwork told a young woman that he could help her become the best known living female artist in all England. He saw in her work the eye, the skill and the sensitivity to become great. She believed him and began following his guidance. During her studies, Ruskin adjusted his evaluation deciding that "she would become the greatest living painter and do things that would be Immortal." As her work improved so did her sensitivity to the work of God in her heart. The Words of God became a powerful influence. At a meeting in London she was challenged to follow God's into a ministry reaching out to young women caught up in trafficking. Although fearful, she followed that calling believing that God could keep her safe.

As her immersion in painting deepened so did her commitment to her spiritual leading. Eventually her mentor John Ruskin complained that her work in London was affecting the quality of her art. He pressed her to make a choice.

Her decision was to leave the tutelage of John Ruskin to follow God. Single and without the support of a mission board using her own resources, she set off for Algiers where she knew no one nor a single word of Arabic.

Her name was Lilias Trotter. Most people have never heard it.

Never hailed as one of the great artists yet over the next four decades, from her base in Algiers, Lilias set up stations along the coast of North Africa and deeper south into the Sahara desert. Scouting areas never before visited by a European woman, often by camel she spent the rest of her life bringing the light and life of the Words of God to the people of North Africa.

Ideas to talk about:
1. **In what ways was Beth following Aleph in the Story?**
2. **Who have you followed and why?**
3. **Do you believe it is worth following God's leadership?**

◊◊◊

(Did the artist lady ever get a tattoo?)

No I don't think so.

(I wanted to get a tattoo once)

You might want to reconsider that.

(Why?)

Following God means checking with Him before we do anything important.

(Is a tattoo such a big deal?)

It could be. He created us. Our bodies belong to Him. it might be a good idea to check with the landlord before spraying graffiti on the building.

(That's funny.)

Chuckle, Yes but true.

Preparation for next week:
- **Read & think about Psalm 119: 41 - 72**
  (Chapters: Vau, Zayin, Heth, Teth)
- **Create a secret Alphabet that only you and God can understand**
- **Write some of your prayers and thoughts to God in your secret**
  language.

◊◊◊

(Creating a secret alphabet sounds like really hard)

It isn't. All you have to do is write out the alphabet and put a different letter or symbol next to it. That becomes your 'code' to write something only God, or someone special can read.

PRAYERS, DREAMS AND HOPES:

WEEK FIVE - God is Good.

Psalm 119: 41-72 (Letters: Vau, Zayin, Heth, Teth)
Rebellion, Guilt, Shame and Gratitude

PRAYER: *"LORD, help me believe that you love me with your trustworthy love."* **Vs. 41**

Read this story aloud:

 **REBELLION**

I heard a huge crash from the upstairs bedroom followed by the sound of breaking glass. A friend my wife had known in High School had just dropped in to stay with us for a time while she got her life sorted out.

Sandy had come from a troubled home and we had not heard from her in many years. Although she had attended church and heard the offer that God makes to any who will receive them, she decided to rebell and go her own way. Stories of alcohol, drugs, and abusive boyfriends would filter back to us. We tried often to reach out. We wondered if we would ever see Sandy again. It took four years.

"Sandy," I mumbled at two am when I opened the door in the middle of a snow storm. She looked really rough. "It's a surprise to see you."

"Yeah. I'm sorry to… Like I wouldn't really bother you but I am broke. Don't have a place to stay."

"Come on in. We have a spare room."

Getting the guest room ready, I told her about God's blessing of finding the beautiful four poster bed last week on a rubbish pile, broken yet easily repaired.

"You get all the luck" came out of her angrily, "I never get s***!

"Sandy, I believe God had this bed set out for you. It's yours if you want it."
Feeding her, getting her and our kids settled down and crawling back in bed, I finally was drifted off to sleep.

Then crash! I ran upstairs, opened the door to find Sandy had kicked the the newly repaired bed frame into pieces and was trying to throw it out the broken window into the snow.

"If it's mine," Sandy yelled, "then I can do anything I want to with it!"
Sandy only stayed a couple of days and moved on.

I still remember that night and how typical it is of how we often treat the gifts that God gives us. It is one thing to do things in ignorance, but too often we have been given wonderful gifts that we reject. When we know the truth and rebel against it, the consequences can be painful.

◊◊◊

(I am learning that, but I cried when I read about Sandy.)

My wife and I cried too.

(Did you ever hear from her again?)

No, but we prayed for her often over the years. God is is her hope. He is never far away.

Ideas to talk about:
1. **When did Beth rebel and make bad choices and what was the result?**
2. **Have you made bad choices that had negative consequences?**

Read this story aloud:

FAILURE

Failure is part of every life.

During an extended stay in Las Vegas for a show, I met Star (not her real name). Ten years of her life were spent there working as a prostitute. After running away from home she had been picked up by a pimp who introduced her to hard drugs, groomed, trafficked and threatened her with horrible consequences if she ever left his stable of young women.

Standing in the Venetian Casino, Star told me about how a kind woman stopped her one night and shared the love of God with her and told of the forgiveness she could find in him. It gave her the courage to confront her 'handler' and leave a destructive life of bondage. She was even given the power to forgive him.

It was the Words of God in Psalm 119 that emboldened her to sand firm. *"Remember your promise to me, your servant. It's my only hope. That is what gives me courage in my misery. Your promise keeps me going."* Vs. 49,50 Then she told me about the ministry she had started to help other young women find freedom. When we fail, there are consequences but God is at work in our failures and in the hard things that result. The good news is that failure is not permanent. We have the grace and forgiveness of God to lift us up and set us back on the path of life.

Ideas to talk about:
1. **Did Beth go through a time of failure?**
2. **Do you feel like you have failed?**

Read this section aloud

3 **SHAME**

It is important to know the difference between guilt and shame. Guilt is the feeling we have when we have done something wrong. It is a prompting from the spirit of God out of a guilty conscience. God provides forgiveness for that.

Shame is how we feel about ourselves. Shame is the negative emotion that declares us worthless, without hope and says to us that we are a failure. It is most often when we others focus on our failures and criticize the unchangeable parts of our lives that create shame on us. Our physical appearance, our family, our past decisions and failures are things we cannot un-change. Believing that is what defines us is shame.

We find forgiveness in God's provision for our sins.

We find freedom from shame in the everlasting, unchanging love of God.

In Psalm 119: 41- 72 we read about how to defend against those who bully or heap shame on you. Here are five admonitions about shame.

1. Give a gentle answer. Speak up kindly when we are shamed or put down. *"rescue me as you promised. Then I can reply to those who make fun of me,"* Vs. 41, 42.

2. Reject shame. Know that God has a purpose for every weakness and failure. *"I will instruct even kings about your laws—I will not be ashamed."* Vs. 46

3. Don't turn away from His Words. Don't let proud people turn you away from God. *"Arrogant people make fun of me, but I don't turn away from your teachings."* Vs. 51

4. Remain attached to God. When you are tempted, stay firmly connected to God. *"Even though wicked people try to tempt me, I will stay attached to your instructions."* Vs. 61

5. Accept discipline. This is a hard one. Discipline is the way God gets our attention and points us back to himself.

"Previously I wandered away from you until you disciplined me, now I listen to what you say." Vs. 67

"The suffering I went through was good for me, so I could think about what you

have taught me." Vs. 71

Ideas to talk about:
1. **Did Beth go through a time when she was bullied or shamed?**
2. **Have you ever been bullied or shamed?**
3. **Have you ever felt that you were disciplined by God?**

◊◊◊

(Some people still bully me. And I know that God has disciplined me. It is a hard to go through.)

Yes it is.

(Have you been disciplined by God?)

It is not something I like talking about but I am very grateful for His discipline. Some of my most valuable lessons were learned through discipline.

4 GRATITUDE

One of my high school friends was the daughter of a very wealthy family. They owned a beautiful estate in Coral Gables Florida and two vacation homes. One in the mountains of Colorado for skiing. One on the beach in the Bahamas. Her name was Erma but I jokingly started calling her Sunny because she was always complaining about something. She was always gloomy. "How," I wondered "could this teenage girl with everything she could possibly ask for including a massive bedroom suite, more clothing than she could wear, travel to elegant places, fancy parties and even her own car be consistently unhappy. Late one evening after a massive birthday party at her parents estate, I met Maria, one of hispanic servants that worked as Sunny's designated chamber maid. She was about the same age. I watched her cleaning up the mess Sunny and her friends had left behind. Humming a happy tune as she worked I got to ask her if she was OK.

"Si, gracias a Dios." she said. 'Yes, thanks be to God.'

Hearing a little bit of her story shed some light on the importance of Gratitude.

"All blessings come from God," she told me. "Even though my Father and mother were killed in the crossfire of a drug war in northern Mexico, my sisters and I managed to escape. I appreciate so much the joy and blessings of having a job, my two sisters and a safe place to live here in the US."

Ideas to talk about:
1. **When did Beth in the story show gratitude?**
2. **What can you be grateful for?**

Preparation for next week:
- **Read & think about Psalm 119: 73 - 104**
  (Chapters: Yodh, Kaph, Lamedh, Mem)
- **Write some things you can be grateful to God for in your journal.**

PRAYERS, DREAMS AND HOPES:

WEEK SIX - God wants you to be strong.

**Psalm 119: 73 -104 (Letters: Yodh, Kaph, Lamedh, Mem)
Power, Healing, Training, Rest**

PRAYER: *"LORD, I pray that your trustworthy love strengthens me as you promised."* **Vs. 76**

1   THE POWER

In 1997 a terrorist group called Boko Haram in Africa kidnapped 240 Girls in the middle of the night from a school in Chebook, Africa. Absolutely terrified, the Girls from 12 -18 years old, were trucked hundreds of miles into the jungle, terrorized, used as hostages, raped, forced into marriages with men much older or who already had one or more wives, and brain washed into accepting a religion that was not their own.

Most of the Girls knew the God of the scriptures and followed Him. Their beloved God gave them the power to stand firm in their faith. Many rejected the indoctrination they were being pressured to accept and suffered for it. In those classes they were given a journal for taking notes about the new beliefs they were being forced into but those remaining true to their faith began writing down verses they remembered from the God's Words. They copied passages from each other from verses they had memorized. One schoolmate had a copy of the "Book of Job." It is the story of a man in the scriptures that was severely tested with endless suffering who refused to renounce his faith. He had the strength to say "Even if I am killed," he said, "I will still trust Him." The girls encouraged each other with these words when the persecution was severe. With the divine power of God's spirit, even under intense pressure, they remained faithful to their God. They too were able to say, "Even if they kill us, we will still trust Him."

◊◊◊

(I really don't think that I could ever say that.)

They did. You could too with the power of God.

Ideas to talk about:
1. **At what point in the story did Beth feel powerful?**
2. **Have you ever felt you needed the power of God?**

2   THE HEALER

Kaph was the healer. When Aleph and Beth arrived at the caves, she provided the salves and bandages for the wounds on their bodies. The very medication Kaph recommended for wounds of the soul was forgiveness.

This is a funny true story. Quite a few years ago I learned a bit about caring for wounds. My mother who was 92 and still on the road with my stepdad, stopped in for a few nights on their annual journey to Florida. I noticed a black and blue area on her left shin that had some kind of a makeshift bandage on it.

"Mom, what is going on with your leg. Can I take a look at it?"

"Sure honey," she responded cheerfully. "I fell about a week ago trying to climb over some railroad ties and cut a gash in my shin." I sat her down in a kitchen chair, got our first aid kit, some clean towels and a bowl of warm water. As I began sponging the area and pealing off what was obviously scotch tape. Covering the wound was a folded piece of paper.

"What is this you have stuck onto your cut Mom." She giggled in an embarrassed way.

"Well when I fell, the cut was bleeding heavily so I needed to staunch the flow. The only thing I could find was a Gideon Bible and roll of scotch tape. So I ripped a page out of the Bible and taped it to my wound. It worked pretty well in stopping the flow."

You would have to know my mom to understand this.

Head back, mouth open and eyes rolled toward the ceiling, all I could say was, "Ay Momma, do you even know what passage of scripture you slapped onto your leg?"

After patching her up I carefully unfolded and rinsed the blood coated bible page revealing that she had torn out a passage from Isaiah 53 which in part reads: *"But He was pierced for our rebellion, crushed for our sins. He was beaten so we could be whole. He was whipped so we could be healed."*

Go figure! Out of a choice of about 500 pages, she would pick that one.

What is even more amazing is this very passage reminds us that our souls are healed by His forgiveness and our willingness to forgive others.

◊◊◊

(Your Mom sounds hysterical. Can I meet her someday?)

You will. But she has gone ahead to heaven so you will have to wait a while.

Ideas to talk about:
1.   **Did Beth understand the power of forgiveness?**
2.   **Who do you need to forgive and find healing with?**

3   THE TEACHER

"I will never forget your instructions, for through them you give me life." Vs. 93

Margaret Brittenham Stone started teaching Sunday School classes when she had just graduated from High School. Teachers in the small town of Davidson Tennessee were scarce so she volunteered. She often had up to twenty students from all ages. For years she instructed them in the scriptures, sometimes needing to teach them how to read. She worked as a secretary for the Davidson County Schools system but the young girls she taught were close to her heart. Many of them came from uneducated families working in the coal industry. Poverty made life challenging. Margaret sat with them around the wood burning pot bellied stove and told stories full of truths from God's Words to the many who could not yet read.

After marriage and raising four of her own children she had the free time to turn her stories into books. With silver white hair, apple ruddy cheeks and a sweet smile she came into my office asking for help publishing her books. I had to agree to help since she was my pastors Mom. After reading her first book we had a painful conversation.

"Margaret, I love the stories but the cost of converting them to books is not worth the money. I don't thinks your books will sell." Cheerfully she answered, "Oh, I don't care about the money. I just want to give these books away to young girls that need the wisdom from God's Words."

◇◇◇

(Sounds like Margaret was doing what you did in Love Letters, right?)

Yes she was. In some way she was part of the inspiration to write my book.

(Did you help her get her books published?)

I did. We figured out a way that she could copy her books one at a time and give them away. A few years later she told me stories about young girls that loved her books and learned about God.

(Cool! Did you ever get a copy?)

No, but I hope her granddaughter is still making copies and giving them away.

Ideas to talk about:
1. **What do you think Beth learned from her Teacher ?**
2. **Is there a Teacher in your life that can help you learn from God's Words?**

◇◇◇

(Well, I guess you are.)

I am honored. Start looking for someone close by that can help. Many women like Margaret who know God's Words would love to help you on your journey.

(Thanks, I will do that.)

4   THE REST

Mercy Street was a weekly gathering designed for those struggling with addictions, compulsive behaviors and dysfunctional lives. Evelyn, the young woman standing before me appeared to be anything but dysfunctional. Beautiful, elegant, styled hair, designer leather purse with the obligatory cell phone clipped to it and dressed from the pages of a fashion magazine, she could have been lawyer, Wall Street broker or CEO of her own corporation. But her perfect makeup was now puddled under her eyes and running down her face. As a struggling alcoholic, she longed for peace. A life filled with the hectic pursuit of material gain and the imaginary glory of smashing some glass ceiling had driven her through 80 hour work weeks, three-martini lunches and open-bar corporate business functions into alcoholic bondage. Through the program at AA she had managed to stay sober for two years but was still hungry for more success. Climbing the ladder had given her no peace. Words from Psalm 119:103, my personal story and simple drawing performed for the group, pointed her to the only one that could give her the 'peace that passes all understanding'. *"Your words taste so sweet to me! They are sweeter than honey to my mouth. Vs. 103"* She wept because now she knew how to find peace.

Ideas to talk about:
1. **Where did Beth find rest?**
2. **Do you know how to find rest in God?**

◊◊◊

(I really am learning. Nightmares used to wake me up every night.

I haven't had one in weeks.)

That is such an encouragement to me and others you can share

with.

Preparation for next week:
-   **Read & think about Psalm 119: 105 - 136**
    (Chapters: Yodh, Kaph, Lamedh, Mem)
-   **See if you can find a Teacher to help you learn more from**
God's
    Words.

PRAYERS, DREAMS AND HOPES:

Psalm 119: 105 - 136 (Letters: Nun, Samech, Ain, Pe)
Scars, Safety, Insight and Leading.

PRAYER: *"LORD, I pray that you will keep me safe, defend me safety and give me wisdom as you said in your words."* Vs. 114

 **SCARS**

"Lord, I am really suffering! Please let me live, as you have promised." Vs. 107

Belinda was born with a tumor on her cheek. By the time she was nine, the growth had disfigured the entire left side of her face. Honduras where she lived, didn't have the Doctors capable of doing the surgery she needed. The tumor would eventually blind one eye, compromise her air passage and take her life.

When the medical team I was traveling with met her, she was too bashful to look anyone in the eye. Her long black hair was always combed to cover the right side of her face. The team resolved to help her.

It took seven years and thirteen surgeries performed at Vanderbilt Hospital to halt the growth. Further surgeries were no longer life saving, they were only cosmetic. I had began calling her Cinderella. She knew the story and had two sisters but I told her that some day her prince would come. Although the scars from the surgery are still evident, Belinda had changed. The shy soft spoken girl, afraid to show her face began to be bold. She started sharing her story publicly explaining that her scars were evidence of God's love for her. Young women especially those who felt ugly were amazed at her grace and confidence. Everyone she met was spiritually impacted by this girl with scars on her face. Being around Belinda was a breath of fresh air.

Taking over her mothers Sunday school class it grew from eight to two-hundred children. She started College, began leading a women's discipleship class and conducted seminars around Honduras. Her message was the same; God loves you no matter what you look like and your scars visible or not can be the most important part of your story.

Then her Prince showed up. Belinda fell in love with Tony, a young man who loved her back just the way she was. They married, had two children and began to tell their story together. The story that God can do something amazing through the scars we bear.

Ideas to talk about:
1. **How did Beth get her scars and who was helped by them?**
2. **Do you have scars visible or not that you feel like hiding?**
3. **How could your scars help someone else?**

◊◊◊

(I have always thought I was ugly, but God is changing my mind.)

That is so good since God did make you exactly the way he wanted you to be.

2 SAFETY

I really don't remember her name. it was a long time ago but she was running away from someone. When she ran across the intersection in front of our car I noticed she had no shoes on and her right foot was bleeding. She looked about fourteen years old. A fast food restaurant was the closest place to hide. My wife and I pulled into the parking lot and walked in as if we were customers stopping for lunch. The girl was in the farthest booth head down with her back to the door. I bought three meals while my wife walked over and sat next to her. When my wife looked back at me and nodded her head, I brought the meals over and sat down. The girl ate like she was starving. Between bites she told us of running away from a foster home where she was kept locked up and abused. The system had failed her. She had gotten a letter from an aunt and uncle in Florida telling her she could come live with them. After escaping she was hitchhiking to get there. Twice men had picked her up and tried to take advantage of her. She felt safe with us.

Taking the folded letter out of her pocket, she gave us her aunts name, address and we tracked down her phone number. I called and spoke to a very kind woman who was mortified that her niece had been placed in such a horrible situation. The aunt understood my caution and was glad to give me names and references that checked out. It was a long drive but we dropped her off in a safe place.

Finding a safe place can sometimes be hard but If you have parents or family that are good to you, that can be the safest place of all.

Ideas to talk about:
1. **Where did Beth feel safe?**
2. **Do you have a safe place to stay?**
3. **If not, who do you know that could help you find a safe place?**

3️⃣ INSIGHT

"Please give me insight, so I can understand your instructions."
Vs.125

Nobody was supposed to know that we were meeting secretly. Her father was very strict and her mother even had spies in the school that reported back to make sure she was not meeting any boys, much less a kid from a different culture and spoke a language they did not speak. We met on the school bus and began passing notes back and forth hoping that no-one would catch us. The day came when one of the spies, her older sister in fact, intercepted my very romantic letter. From that point on we were watched like criminals. Discovering new ways of passing our words and feelings to each other became an obsession. One of my favorites was taking a large rubber band. Stretching it all the way across my biggest textbook and writing on it with a ball point pen worked. When the rubber band was released all the letters shrunk down to tiny horizontal lines that you couldn't read. I could even shoot it across the class room to her. She would stretch the rubber band back out and read it all. It was amazing how much we could write on one rubber band.

Eventually I devised a secret code. I could write in between the lines of books in the library and she would write back. The code was like a foreign language that no one could read but us. As sometimes happens, over the years, we lost touch.

Most of the Love Letters God has written for us were written in an alphabet called Hebrew. You probably don't know that ancient language but God *has* written his words in a profound spiritual way that reveals messages for you. If you look for them.

◊◊◊

(Did that girl ever write you again?)

No, but if she does, I still have the secret code.

(Can I really find hidden messages from God?)

I believe it to be true and have read many verses that seemed as if God wrote them for me alone.

Ideas to talk about:

1. How did Beth discover the secret language?
2. Do you recognize any of the Hebrew letters?
3. Has anyone ever written to you in a secret language?

4   LEADING

"Studying your words brings light." Vs. 130 "Lead me by your word in the way I should go." Vs. 133

Do you remember me telling you about Cindy, my Glad Girl? Anyway, she regularly tells me when she feels God wants us to do something. As I finished the book 'Love Letters,' she said, "Joe, I think we should give all the money that comes in from the sale of this book to a ministry that helps young girls."

"All of it?" I asked a little nervously. COVID19 had just shut down the country and all of my work had gone away. There was no way of knowing if I would every get another job. I started writing the book because I didn't have much to do. "Are you sure we should give it all away?" I asked again.

Now Cindy, my 'Glad Girl' doesn't claim to hear God's words audibly yet she walks with Him daily and faithfully reads and pays attention to His Words. Her copy of the Scriptures is underlined and she writes down what God wants her to do. As far as I have been able to determine in twenty four years of marriage, she has never been led astray.

She told me, "God leads us everyday. Don't you think He will keep doing it?"

(Yeah, Mr. Spiritual. She told you to put your money where your mouth was.)

Yes she did. And she was right. God has continued to provide for us every day.

(I would quit reading this Study Guide if you hadn't listened to her.)

Don't do that. God will still be faithful even if I am not.

Ideas to talk about:
1. **In 'Love Letters,' how did the light help them find their way?**
2. **Have you ever felt God leading you?**

Preparation for next week:
- **Read & think about Psalm 119: 137 - 176 (Chapters: Tzaddi, Qoph, Resh, Shin)**
- **Devise a 'Secret Aleph-Bet' that you can use to write to someone   in secret.**
- **Write a note to someone in your secret Aleph-Bet. (You need to send them a copy of the code.)**

(Wow, that sounds hard. I don't think I can do that.)

Sure you can. Just write the alphabet in a vertical column and assign a number, letter or symbol to each one.

PRAYERS, DREAMS AND HOPES:

WEEK EIGHT - God is Just,

**Psalm 119: 137 - 168 (Letters: Tzaddi, Qoph, Resh, Shin)
Justice, Holiness, Truth, Battles**

PRAYER: *"LORD, help me see your word with awe for your word is truth, It will last forever."* Vs. 160

1 JUSTICE

"Lord you are right and what you decide is just!" Vs. 137

Cory and Betsy were young women forced to live under Nazi rule when Hitler invaded Holland. They along with their father Casper ten Boom, began rescuing the Jews that were being deported to the prison camps. Eventually the were caught and subjected to the same torment and were deported to the death camp at Ravensbrook. Even suffering horribly they, like the girls of Chibook, trusted God to do the right thing. Betsy would quote *"Your instructions are fair and totally just." Vs. 138* During that time it was Betsy that kept repeating, *"There is no pit so deep that God is not deeper still."* After years of suffering God took Betsy home to Heaven. At the right time God brought justice upon the Nazi regime.

He had a different plan for Cory. It was the other side of Justice. Judgement must be brought to bear for those who do wrong, but Judgement alone can be cruel. Parents and all those in authority must show Mercy along with justice. That is the grace that motivated Cory to do what she did after being released from the prison camp. Cory began traveling the world telling the story of God's immeasurable Grace and how they found the light of God in the darkest of all places.

Ideas to talk about:
1. **When was Beth given the opportunity to bring judgement on the guilty?**
2. **Are you in a situation where you feel you want justice?**

2 MERCY

"My whole being is crying out for your mercy. Lord, please answer me!" Vs. 145

Cory Ten-Boom, having seen the darkest of inhumanity had been given Mercy. She was released from the death camp by a miraculous clerical mistake and knew that her mission was to go out and spread the message of God's Mercy to those who had been crushed by the Nazi boot. In meeting after meeting she shared her story of how God had supported them in Ravensbrook and how she had learned the value and importance of forgiveness.

One night she concluded her remarks by saying God had showed her his mercy and she was now sharing it with those who had captured and tortured her. At that moment from the back of the room a man arose moving toward the front. She recognized him. He was one of the Nazi guards at Ravensbrook partially responsible for the deaths of thousands. He was responsible for the suffering and death of her sister Betsy. In her own words she wrote later.

"I remembered him and the leather crop swinging from his belt. It was the first time since my release that I had been face to face with one of my captors and my blood seemed to freeze."

"You mentioned Ravensbrück in your talk,' he was saying. 'I was a guard in there. But since that time, I know that God has forgiven me for the cruel things I did, but I would like to hear it from your lips as well." He extended his hand. "will you forgive me?"

"I wrestled with the most difficult thing I had ever had to do. I knew that God wanted me to forgive him."

"Still I stood there with the coldness clutching my heart. But forgiveness is not an emotion–I knew that too. Forgiveness is an act of the will, and the will can function regardless of the feelings in your heart, Woodenly, mechanically, I thrust my hand into the one stretched out to me. As I did, an incredible thing took place. The current started in my shoulder, raced down my arm, sprang into our joined hands. And then this healing warmth seemed to flood my whole being, bringing tears to my eyes.

"I forgive you, brother!" I cried. "With all my heart!"

I had never known God's love so intensely as I did then."

Ideas to talk about:
1. **Did Beth learn about mercy and forgiveness?**
2. **Who do you need to show Mercy to and forgive?**

3   TRUTH

"Your word can be summed up in one word: Truth!" Vs. 160

Joan was born in France, the daughter of a poor farmers who raised her to love God. At the age of sixteen she courageously took up weapons and encouraged the French army to defend themselves against invaders who had taken a large portion of their country and held it under siege. Before starting out to attack the enemy she had her standard painted with an image of Christ in Judgment and a banner made bearing the name of Jesus. The discouraged, defeated army were encouraged by the standard and were victorious in battle led by Joan who became known as the Maid of Orleans.

A flag, is a symbol or logo that represents the most important thing about who we are and what you do. Beth's Banner, called Resh, was the standard that represented TRUTH. God has set his Words as the standard we follow. These words of love that are considered 'Truth.'

Ideas to talk about:
1. **How important was the banner 'Resh' to the soldiers Beth led?**
2. **Do you have a hard time telling the TRUTH?**

4   THE BATTLE

"Princes attack me for no reason, but I am in awe of your word."

Sitting back stage at the America's Got Talent tryouts I watched Skilyr, a young fourteen year old girl lift her naturally beautiful voice above the cheering audience then hand it gently to the three judges wide eyed in amazement. Immediately she was passed on to the next round. It was a gift.

Every life has its battles. All achievement requires a conquest. You move forward by struggling against gravity, inertia and failure. My conversations during AGT with other contestants often involved stories of hard work, intense highs and devastating lows. We bonded over our shared battles that included a balance of misery and success.

Years later a news report told of how Skilyr success had changed her. Fame, wealth and pride caused division and angry fights among family and friends that led her downward into addiction. It became a battle she could not win. At the last she died of a suspected drug overdose at the young age of twenty three. This was a great tragedy. Reading about it reminded me about how victory is won each day in small battles with small choices guided by the wisdom contained in the Words of God. It is a steadfast faith in God and the invincible power of His Spirit and His Word's that gives us the victory.

Ideas to talk about:

1. **What was the biggest battle Beth faced?**
2. **What battles are you facing?**

Preparation for next week:

about Psalm 119: 169 - 176
(One Chapter: Tav)
Write down and be ready to share next week, what has been the best part of your journey.

◊◊◊

(Do I have to pick just one?)

You can always write more. I hope writing in your journal will become a permanent part of your life.

PRAYERS, DREAMS AND HOPES:

WEEK NINE - God gives you Joy.

Psalm 119: 169 - 176 (The Letter: Tav)
He will save you and give you Salvation, Victory, Praise, Joy

PRAYER: *"LORD, save me as you promised and I will pour out words of praise."* **Vs. 170, 171**

1 **SALVATION**

"Please hear what I am saying to you and save me as you promised." Vs. 170

Downtown Detroit was a mess. Abandoned, graffiti-spattered brick buildings looked down on me from broken out windows. A small group of people stood with the empty eyed look of the buildings I had walked past; empty, homeless, hopeless, in front of a stone church with stained glass windows. "Spirit of Hope, Everybody Eats," was hand-painted on a sign leaning up against the wrought iron gate. That was where I met Emily. An open door spilled aromas of hot food. Inside a shorthanded group of volunteers filled plates, handed out trays, cool-aid and smiles. "Thanks for coming." "Need another helping?" "Glad to see you today." Emily was coordinating the group.

I volunteered working alongside Emily. She was twenty two… maybe. A struggling artist that had moved into dilapidated 'Crow Manor,' the artist commune next door. Selling hand made jewelry was her only means of support. Her story was a sad tale of getting kicked beaten and rejected. Running away. Running again. Finally running into Pastor John at the Spirit of Hope church. There she found Hope. She found Salvation and rescue from her depression and despair. First she just needed to receive. To heal. To hear about the Savior. Then slowly began to contribute. It was a good story.

After the last pot had been washed, Emily showed me around back where she pulled weeds, tended, harvested an overflowing garden. It was an abandoned lot that tilled, watered, planted, cared for, was yielding a harvest. Growing the spirit of hope. Downtown Detroit was being redeemed one empty lot, one abandoned house, one recycled church, one broken life at time.

1. Have you received God's Salvation?
2. Can you share your story with someone who needs to hear it?

2   VICTORY

"Please hear what I have to say and give me victory as you promised." Vs. 170

Ella fought more battles than almost anyone I know. She fought a miserable childhood filled with every kind of abuse. For many years she battled the emotional scars of rejection and loneliness. The war continued with a recurring skirmish with cancer, surgery and chemotherapy. An unfortunate marriage and divorce renewed the struggle brought on by divorce, poverty, homelessness with the additional burden of raising two girls as a single mother. In the midst of it all she fought her way up the educational hill Eventually she got her Masters degree, taught school, providing for herself and two daughters. After buying her own home, given one of the highest awards her school board offered she paused to reflect. She could finally catch her breath, looking back over the detritus strewn battlefield she saw herself not looser but a winner. In every trial, struggle, and battle, God had given her victory not defeat.

Ideas to talk about:
1. **How did you feel reading about Beth's victory?**
2. **Do you remember a time where you experienced victory?**
3. **Who do you know that needs a win?**

3   PRAISE

"Let me pour out my words of praise, for you teach me what to do." Vs. 171

Every part of our lives can be lifted up as worship to God. Praise is a lot like gratitude in action. We sing, we share, we give, we hope, we forgive, we love because he first loved us.

Audrey at eighteen, lost her first husband in the war. Moving back in with her parents, broken hearted, she thought she would never marry again. But watching from a distance, Ralph who had loved her from fifth grade had his heart broken when she had married a guy he knew was bad news. But he waited. At the right

time, knowing he would have to ask Audrey's father, Mr. Eisler if he could marry his daughter. Finally he drummed up enough courage to drop by to help her dad dig a drainage ditch in their back yard. After days of hard digging Ralph taking a break mumbled, "I'd like to marry your daughter."
Without slowing down the pace of his digging, he responded. "Well son, go get her."

The joy of those words not only brought them together but eventually into a praise filled walk with God. Their joy together lasted sixty four years. Ralph eventually became my father-in-law. I don't ever remember either one of them saying an unkind word to anyone. They praised people, praised God and lived lives of Joy.

Ideas to talk about:
1. **Did Beth find opportunities to lift up words of Praise?**
2. **How often do you make time to Praise God?**

JOY

"Lord your teachings give me joy!" Vs. 174

Katherine married Jay right after college and moved to LA to pursue their dreams--she as a model and he as a lawyer. Just six months later everything changed. Katherine collapsed without warning suffering a massive stroke. Though her chance of survival was slim she was rushed into brain surgery. Katherine survived the removal of part of her brain. Her future recovery was unsure yet there was a spark of hope. Forty days on life support in the ICU and nearly two years in full-time brain rehab, resulted in '*Hope Heals*' the story of Katherine and Jay's struggle to restore Katherine's quality of life. She was forced to learn how to talk, eat, and walk. With a severely disabled body Katherine and Jay in the midst of continuing hardship committed to celebrating this gift of a second chance by embracing a life of Joy. Watching her speak on stage from a wheel chair, her message peppered with quotes from God's Words, is filled with JOY.

◊◊◊

(I get it! Everything doesn't get fixed today. Life isn't always peachy but God gave us all the instructions we need in His Words.)

It sounds to me like you have really understood what he wanted you to know. Well done lady!

(Thank You)

You are on your way to a joyful future and God gets all the credit.

PRAYERS, DREAMS AND HOPES:

For the Group Leader

This is a profound and comprehensive study of Psalm 119.
based on the fictional novel, 'Love Letters.' It can be covered in sections based on the abilities of your group to comprehend and the time allotted for the study. Each chapter is divided into four sections which could be studied independently of the others. The topics covered are listed here.
True stories of young women and their struggles are included in each topic to illustrate the way God's Words can impact lives in the real world.

Chapter 1 Vs. 1
- Words, Symbols, Provision, Heart
Chapter 2 Vs. 2 - 8
- Your Value, Your Name, Your New Name, God's Name
Chapter 3 Vs. 9 - 16
- Study the Word, Enjoy the Word, Memorize the Word, Share the Word
Chapter 4 Vs. 17 - 40
- Discover, Understand, Trust, Follow
Chapter 5 Vs. 41 - 72
- Rebellion, Guilt, Shame, Gratitude
Chapter 6 Vs. 73 - 104
- Power, Healing, Training, Rest
Chapter 7 Vs. 105 - 136
- Scars, Safety, Insight, Leading
Chapter 8 Vs. 137 - 168
- Justice, Holiness, Truth, The Battle
Chapter 9 Vs. 169 - 176
- Victory, Salvation, Praise, Joy

The Author:
Joe S. Castillo

I love a good story!

    I write, share, paint, and create stories in sand for live audiences.

    Mexico City was where I was born, grew up and learned to love art and stories.

    The schools I almost flunked out of, were three High Schools, Ringling College of Art and Design, Florida Bible College and Asbury Seminary.

    Many of the hats I have worn include: advertiser, publisher, pastor, entrepreneur, writer, artist and storyteller. I now wear a beret and …

I wrote this story for you.

    My "storytelling artwork" was born out of a struggle to forgive which I wrote about in my first book, *The Face of Christ. JoeCastillo.com*

    SandStory has been my greatest adventure in Storytelling. I use sand, light and music to engage and inspire audiences all over the world. SandStory.com

    These stories have been performed in over twenty countries for churches, conferences, Fortune 500 companies, world leaders, CBS, NBC, the BBC and reached the finals on America's Got Talent.

    I am married to my "Glad Girl", Cindy, have four kids, eight grandkids and love living just south of Atlanta, Georgia in a new town for creatives called Trilith.

    If you are nearby,
stop and visit.

I have four other books available wherever books are sold.
- The Face of Christ - An amazing story of loss forgiveness and restoration.
- SandStory - How ordinary sand changed my life.
- Love Letters - (for Young Women) Search with all your heart.
- Escape - (for Boys and Young Men) Snares, Traps and how to escape them.

Enjoy the journey!